For Baby G., with all my love. You're in our hearts always.
—L.G.

STERLING CHILDREN'S BOOKS
New York

An Imprint of Sterling Publishing Co., Inc.
1166 Avenue of the Americas
New York, NY 10036

ISBN 978-1-4549-2511-8

Distributed in Canada by Sterling Publishing Co., Inc.
c/o Canadian Manda Group, 664 Annette Street
Toronto, Ontario, M6S 2C8, Canada
Distributed in the United Kingdom by GMC Distribution Services
Castle Place, 166 High Street, Lewes, East Sussex, BN7 1XU, England
Distributed in Australia by NewSouth Books
45 Beach Street, Coogee, NSW 2034, Australia

For information about custom editions, special sales, and premium and corporate purchases,
please contact Sterling Special Sales at 800-805-5489 or specialsales@sterlingpublishing.com.

Manufactured in China

Lot #:
10 9 8 7 6 5 4 3 2 1

11/18

sterlingpublishing.com

Cover and Interior design by Irene Vandervoort

A Couch for
LLAMA

Leah Gilbert

STERLING CHILDREN'S BOOKS
New York

The Lago family's couch
was very
well-loved.

It was the perfect spot for snuggling and reading,

card playing,
fort building, and
hiding and seeking!

They had
many good
times together.

Maybe a few
TOO MANY
good times . . .

WHEE!

OOPS!

HEY!

One day they realized it was time for a new couch.

So they piled into the family car
and off they went to find one.

One that was not
TOO BIG.

Or

TOO SMALL.

But JUST RIGHT.

The Lago family found the perfect couch.

But on the way home,
something went wrong.

whoosh!

Llama found a couch.

Llama brayed
"HELLO!"
to the couch.

But the couch
didn't say
anything.

Llama tried to share his lunch,
but the couch didn't seem
to have much of an appetite.

So Llama ate the couch instead.

It tasted worse than
a dry,
dusty
TUMBLEWEED.

The couch was useless!

TAKE IT AWAY!

But it just

wouldn't **budge.**

The Lago family noticed something was missing.

Meanwhile, Llama decided to just ignore
the couch and pretend it wasn't there.

This got
VERY,
VERY
BORING.

So Llama snuck up
and
POUNCED,

and
BOUNCEY-
BOUNCEY-
BOUNCED,

WHIRLED

and

JUMPED...

and

TWIRLED,

BUMPED

And fell down
into the
smooshy-mooshy,
fluffy-puffy
cushions.

He actually finally,
completely

LOVED
the couch.

The Lago family found their couch.
And also
A LLAMA!

Specifically, a **stubborn,** couch-loving
kind of llama.

They had a **great idea...**

At the end of the day, the Lago family
was happy with their new couch . . .

But Llama
was the
happiest
of all.